Spiral

K.L. Denman

orca soundings

ORCA BOOK PUBLISHERS

Copyright © 2007 K.L. Denman

All rights reserved. No part of this publication may be reproduced or transmitted in any form or by any means, electronic or mechanical, including photocopying, recording or by any information storage and retrieval system now known or to be invented, without permission in writing from the publisher.

Library and Archives Canada Cataloguing in Publication

Denman, K.L., 1957-
Spiral / written by K.L. Denman.
(Orca soundings)

ISBN 978-1-55143-932-7 (bound).--ISBN 978-1-55143-930-3 (pbk.)

I. Title. II. Series.
PS8607.E64S65 2008   jC813'.6   C2008-903132-6

First published in the United States, 2008
Library of Congress Control Number: 2008928861

Summary: After breaking her back, fifteen-year-old Abby tries everything to take away her pain before finding the answer in a patient horse called Charlie and learning to have faith in herself.

Orca Book Publishers is dedicated to preserving the environment and has printed this book on paper certified by the Forest Stewardship Council.®

Orca Book Publishers gratefully acknowledges the support for its publishing programs provided by the following agencies: the Government of Canada through the Canada Book Fund and the Canada Council for the Arts, and the Province of British Columbia through the BC Arts Council and the Book Publishing Tax Credit.

Cover photography by Corbis Images

ORCA BOOK PUBLISHERS
PO Box 5626, Stn. B
Victoria, BC Canada
V8R 6S4

ORCA BOOK PUBLISHERS
PO Box 468
Custer, WA USA
98240-0468

www.orcabook.com
Printed and bound in Canada.

14 13 12 11 • 5 4 3 2

*For Tiffany and her beloved horses,
Frosty and Shania.*

*Far back,
far back in our dark soul
the horse prances.*
—D.H. Lawrence

Chapter One

I wasn't always a cripple. There was a time when I was a regular girl, fifteen years old, going to school, hanging out with friends, playing soccer, doing whatever kids do. I had a boyfriend. I had a family. I got a job.

I got a job. Yeah, it was good. I wanted extra spending money, cash for new clothes and movies and makeup.

Maybe save up enough to buy a car. My friends said I was lucky because I wasn't washing dishes or bagging groceries. I was a display assistant in a furniture store, and I helped set up little fake rooms. This was a major score because I totally wanted to be an interior decorator.

There was a catch. The catch was my boss, Ms. Trent, who couldn't crack a smile if her life depended on it. Or if my life depended on it. She snapped orders like an army sergeant. "C'mon, hustle. We haven't got all day. Move it, kid."

Kid. I wonder if she even knew my name. Couldn't she have said, "Move it, Abby"?

So that day, when Ms. Trent pointed at the ceiling and said, "Go up there and change that lightbulb and make it quick," I didn't argue. I got the ladder. I set it up against the shelving unit. I climbed to the top, and when I couldn't reach the light socket, I crawled onto the shelving. I knelt and still couldn't reach, so I crouched, stood...and everything started to sway.

And then I was falling. It was like being in one of those dreams where you're free-falling, and you want to scream but you have no breath. And don't you always wake up before you hit bottom? Someone once told me we do, because if we don't wake up, we die, right there in our sleep. I didn't die. But the only thing between me and the concrete floor was the metal shelving, the unit that collapsed. The one I shouldn't have been standing on. Falling backward onto that broke my back. So say the doctors.

The doctors say a lot of things. They say I'm lucky to be alive. They say I'm lucky the shelves didn't hit my spinal column higher up, at the neck.

Then I'd be a quadriplegic instead of a paraplegic.

"Yeah, right," I say. "I'm just like that lost dog."

"I don't understand," the doctor replies. His brows gather into a knot.

"C'mon," I scoff. "There's me, lucky to get a job, lucky to be alive, lucky I'm not a quadriplegic. And then there's that poster. You know the one. Lost Dog. Three legs, blind in left eye, missing an ear, accidentally neutered. Answers to the name of Lucky." I stare at him.

He doesn't laugh. His brows smooth out and he sighs. "Listen, Abby. I know how hard this must be for you."

I'm the one who laughs. "Right. You know how it feels to be told you'll never walk again?"

"Sorry," he says. "I shouldn't have said it quite like that. How's your pain level? Do you need a shot?"

Spiral

I turn away. This is what they do. They can't find the right words to say, and they wimp out, dope me up, shut me up. I know it's crazy to be angry with them, it's not their fault. But I can't seem to help it.

Fault. My parents are into that. They sat beside my bed and wept and held my hand and washed me and brushed my hair and positioned the vile bedpan and cried. Then one day, my dad went nuts.

"Stupid greedy piece of scum! She risks my daughter for a lightbulb? Sends you up a ladder onto her junk shelving? She has no safety rules in place, does she? It's all about the money, isn't it? Squeeze every scrap of time out of a body with no regard for proper training, no proper equipment! We are going to sue that miserable excuse for a human being. She's going to pay for this!"

He pauses to draw breath, and my mom puts a hand on his arm. Softly, she says, "I've already looked into that, dear."

His crazed stare slowly focuses on her. "You have?"

"Yes. We can't sue. Abby can get some compensation from the government plan for workers, but...the employer is protected."

Dad's eyes bulge outward. His jaw drops open. "The...the *employer* is protected?" His right hand forms a fist and it slams into his left palm. Smack. "Well," he says. "Well. We'll see about that."

The next day, he makes a huge sign and takes it to the furniture store. He walks up and down on the sidewalk in front of that store all day. And the next day. And the next. Mom tells me people stop and talk to him. It takes a while, but I finally get her to tell me what's written on his sign. It says *Life-Changing Work.*

I say, "Huh?"

Mom shakes her head. "He couldn't write anything that defames the store, or they'd be the ones suing him. This way, people ask him questions. Then he tells them what happened to you."

"Oh."

"He even attracted some media. One of the TV stations wants to interview you..."

"What? No!"

"Don't worry. He refused."

Dad keeps at it for weeks. When he hears that Ms. Trent no longer works at the furniture store, he stops. He comes by for a visit and says, "I thought it might make it hurt less. But it doesn't."

None of us hurt less. There is only a weary, half-assed acceptance. And under that, under the heart that still beats in my chest, in that half of me with sensation, there is a boulder of anger. A massive, cold, heavy boulder of anger.

Chapter Two

They send me to rehab. I'm supposed to learn how to live my life in a wheelchair. Right. I can *live* like this? I go along with their routine. They teach me exercises, proper nutrition, how to keep my butt from getting bedsores. Wow. So very cool.

When my boyfriend, Todd, comes by, I dump him. I say, "You know, Todd,

I never realized what a bore you are. I mean, now that all we can do is sit around and talk, I've found out you're pretty stupid."

Todd's face goes red. Tears waver in his blue eyes. God, I love those blue eyes. He puts a hand on my knee, which I can't feel, and says, "Abby. Come on. Don't be like this. Please."

My lip curls into a sneer. "Don't be like this? See, that's what I'm talking about, Todd. This is who I am now, and I can't stand you anymore. Don't you get it? I've changed." I take a breath and add, "Besides, I've met someone else."

"No way!" he sputters. "Who? Where?"

"What, you don't believe me? There are guys in here, Todd. And this one, his name is Jim. He's so sweet and funny and smart." I can't look at Todd when I say this. Jim is the biggest jerk I've ever met. He's the sort of person who laughs when people fall out of wheelchairs.

Todd is silent for a while. Finally, he says, "Abby, you're just doing this because you think I shouldn't be stuck with someone who's…hurt."

He is so right. And he's never going to know that, not if I can help it. "Todd. Don't kid yourself. It's over, okay? We have nothing in common. I don't think we ever did. And trust me, I'm not doing this for you. I'm doing it for me."

And that's true, I am doing it for me.

He says, "But we can still be friends, can't we? I mean, I can still come and hang out, right?"

"Wrong. Just go, Todd. Please, just go."

He stands and shoves his hands into his pockets. His feet shuffle. Then he stoops and kisses the top of my head.

I hear him make this awful little choking sound. And he leaves.

It's almost that easy to get rid of most of my friends. Seems like some of the girls I thought were friends were really just habits. As in, we only hung out because the universe stuck us in the same little corner of the planet. Is it like that for everyone? Our parents pick a place to live, and then we end up together in school, on the same sports teams. Just basically stuck with whoever happens to be there.

It's especially easy when Savannah and Randi come in.

Savannah plops down on my bed, tosses back her hair and says, "So, we were at this party on the weekend, right? And there were all these hot guys."

Randi cuts in. "Yeah, omigod, it was like this whole hockey team."

Savannah glares. "Do you mind, Randi? I was talking." Another hair toss. "So, yeah, anyway, I met this cutie and we got together. I just can't *wait* for him to call." She pauses and adds, "I gave him my number."

"I met one too," Randi says. "And we were grinding, right? Then, in like no time, we started making out and... Oh!" Her hand flies up and covers her mouth. Her mascara-thick lashes start to flutter.

"Idiot!" Savannah hisses.

"I'm sorry," Randi squeaks.

"What?" I ask.

"Well, you know," Savannah says. "I mean, we don't want to upset you."

"Excuse me?" It couldn't have been Todd she was with, could it? No. He always said Randi was about fifty cards short of a deck.

"Duh," says Randi. She flutters her lashes again and whispers, "Sex."

I'm still not quite clued in. "You mean you had sex with this guy at the party?"

Randi grins and nods happily.

"God," I say. "Don't you think that's kind of slutty?"

"See?" says Savannah. "You shouldn't talk about it to her, Randi. I told you."

Randi's lip juts into a pout. "Jeez, it just slipped out, okay?"

I stare at her. "That *easy*, huh?"

"Omigod," Randi says, "you don't have to get like that. Calling me a slut, just because *you* can't do it. Like, *ever*."

I feel like she just dumped a bucket of ice water over my head. I go cold, all over. I start shaking. Then I scream, "You stupid little whore! Get out!"

And they get out.

I can't ditch Lily though. I try. I do the same things I did to the others, tell her to shut up, screw off, whatever it takes. She calls me on it, big time. "Okay, Abby. Go ahead. Be the nastiest you can be. But I'm telling you right now, girlfriend, I am here for you and nothing you say is going to change that."

"Is that right?" I ask. I try hard to sound tough.

"Yeah, that's right," she shoots back. "So are you going to cut the crap or what?"

"You know," I say, "I've always thought that was a weird expression. Who actually cuts crap? How gross is that?"

Lily's nose wrinkles. "Man. That is gross. That is *so* gross."

I can't help it. I start to laugh. Then Lily's laughing too, and her arms go around me and I know there's no way I can win this one. And I'm so damn crazy happy to lose, I start crying. I cry for a long time, and Lily cries too.

When we're done, when our laps are heaped with soggy tissue and we're hiccupping, she lays a hand on my cheek and says, "Thank god for you, Abby. I really need you, you know?"

Chapter Three

We're in the meeting room, sitting in our circle, and as usual, I'm not saying much. Nothing, if I can help it. We're supposed to be sharing our feelings, talking through our trauma, preparing for our release from rehab. There are six in our group, all under the age of twenty-five. There are four guys, including Jim the Jerk, and one other girl.

We've talked about our accidents, how we got here. Two of the others were in car wrecks, one had a snowboarding accident, and, funny, ha ha, three of us are here because of accidents on the job. Who knew working could be so dangerous? Not me.

Mrs. Green, our group leader (a shrink), goes off about that. "Young people are getting injured in the workplace every day. They're losing fingers in meat slicers, losing eyes from splashed chemicals, suffering burns from hot cooking oil. They're ordered to do things without a moment of training. A moment of time on the part of an employer, that's all it would take to prevent so much pain."

Jim says, "So what's up with the workers? Why don't they just tell the boss to go piss up a rope?" Jim broke his back in a car accident. He was driving,

Spiral

speeding, drunk. Acts like he's proud of it.

Mrs. Green frowns. "They don't speak up because they're afraid. It's as simple as that. They think if they refuse to do what they're told, they'll get fired. Sadly, sometimes that's true."

"Better off fired than crippled," I mutter.

"Yes," she agrees. Her voice softens. "But no one expects these things to happen. And young people are trained to obey the adults in charge. Parents control the home, teachers control the school environment. Think about it. Usually, the adults are trying to protect the kids, not asking them to do something dangerous. And the other part of this is that young people don't want to admit when they don't know how to do something. Quite the opposite. Kids will pretend to know what they're doing just to impress a boss or their coworkers."

"So it's their own dumb fault," says Jim.

"No!" Mrs. Green snaps. "It is *not* their fault! The responsibility for safety and training belongs with the employer!"

I've heard this before. I don't want to hear it again. I say, "Do you mind if I go now? I'm tired."

Mrs. Green tilts her head to one side and taps a finger on her lips. "We'll be done soon. Can you hang in a bit longer, Abby?"

I shrug. "I guess so."

Unfortunately, now I've got her attention. "Tell me, Abby, how are you feeling about yourself?"

God, I can't stand this. But instead of my usual shrug, I start talking. "How am I feeling? Gee, hmmm. I feel short. Yeah, that's it. Short."

Spiral

"I see," says Mrs. Green.

"Do you? Really? See, the thing is, I used to feel tall. I'm just a couple inches shy of six feet. Did you know that? Didn't think so. I was tall, and I was used to looking down at most people. Not that it made me feel like I was better than them. It's just the way it was. The view I knew. And now? Well, now I look at bellies and butts."

"And boobs," Jim snickers. "Don't forget the boobs."

"You are such a dick," I say.

"All right." Mrs. Green raises a hand. "Please, let's not lose track of the topic. Now, Abby, you say you feel short. Does that in itself make you less of a person?"

I know what I'm supposed to say. Instead I tell her, "Yes. Yes it does make me less."

"How so?"

"I don't know. It just does."

"Interesting. I'd like to explore this further. How do short people feel about their height? Do you think they feel inferior to others?"

"Look, you're missing the point here. I was tall. Now I'm not. That's it." And then I say, "And when I dumped my boyfriend, when he left, he kissed me on the top of the head." The moment these words leave my mouth, I want to take them back. I can't believe I said this out loud. I cringe, waiting for Jim to laugh. Against all odds, he doesn't.

"Ah," says Mrs. Green. "Okay. You know, Abby, I think what you're feeling is that you've been forced back into the place of a small child. That's a helpless place sometimes, isn't it? Being small and defenceless. Looking up at others."

Mrs. Green leans forward from her wheelchair. "I felt that too. Oh, so fiercely I felt it, and I hated it.

Spiral

But there is a way to overcome it. It will take time, for all of you, but I can tell you, it's possible. What you must strive for is an identity you can own. Find the true you. And when you find that person, nurture him or her. Make that person strong, confident and whole. That sense of self gives you a presence. And when you have *that*... Then short or tall, standing or sitting, others will sense it flowing from you. And they'll know you're their equal."

She sees the doubt on our faces.

"They will," she says.

"So who cares?" Jim asks. "I don't care what anyone else thinks of me."

For once, Jim and I agree.

Chapter Four

I thought going home would be good. It had to be better than rehab. But the first thing that happens is Dad arrives to pick me up in a beige minivan.

"Where's your Mustang?" I ask. Dad's black Mustang was the most pimped-out ride ever.

He shrugs. "I traded it in. I was getting tired of that car. Time for a change."

That's a lie. Dad loved that car.

He keeps talking. "Isn't this lift on the van the neatest gadget? See, you just park on the little ramp, press the button and, zip, up you go."

It gets worse. When we pull up in front of the house, I see that my favorite part of our yard, Mom's herb garden, has disappeared beneath an ugly wooden ramp.

"See that?" Dad asks.

"Kind of hard to miss," I mutter.

"Built it myself," he says proudly.

I try to smile. "Thanks."

"Just wait until you see your new room," he says.

My new room? I love my *old* room. Just five short months ago, a lifetime ago, it was my first interior-decorating project. Mom took me around to garage sales until I found the perfect furniture to refinish. Lily helped me paint. I even managed to sew my own curtains and pillow covers. What had he done? And then it hits me. My room was upstairs.

Up.

Stairs.

Maybe part of my brain was paralyzed in the accident too, because I should have been prepared for this. Did they mention it? I search my memory and do recall some talk about moving my bed…I must have tuned them out.

I let Dad take hold of my wheelchair and roll me up the ugly ramp, over the dead herb garden. I could easily wheel myself, should be doing it. Mrs. Green warned us not to let others take over. But right now my independence seems very far away.

When we get to the top of the ramp, Mom flings open the front door. She's smiling and crying, and my little brother, Will, is standing behind her.

Will is ten, and he's trying to smile but he looks nervous, almost like he's afraid of me. Like I'm a stranger. Weird. He visited often enough when I was in the hospital. He should be used to seeing the new me.

"Hey, Mom," I say. "Hey, Pukeface," I add. That's my nickname for Will, and when he hears it, his face lights up.

"Shut up, Abble," he says. That's his brilliant nickname for me. I give him a shot in the shoulder when I pass by. He tries to give me a noogie in return, but Mom stops him.

"Will! Leave your sister alone."

I give Will a narrow look. "I'll see *you* later."

He sticks out his tongue, and I feel something unfamiliar on my lips. A smile. Maybe it's going to be all right.

And it is, for a week or so. It turns out Dad moved all my furniture down to the den beside the kitchen. None of us had ever used that room much, so at least taking it over doesn't make me feel guilty. He even tried his best to redo my faux paint job, and Mom hung up my pictures and curtains. It looks pretty good. When Lily comes by, she's impressed.

"This is cool, Abby. Close to the food source. Your own phone and computer." She raises an eyebrow. "Even convenient for slipping out the back door to meet your lover."

I snort. "As if that's ever going to happen."

"Never say never," she says softly. "I did some research, Abby. You can still have a full life—including normal relationships and babies. You're what they call a T-10 paraplegic, right? You have a bit of sensation in your lower body, right? Even T-5s, with the injury higher up their back and no sensation farther down, have children. Did you know that?"

"Lily?"

"Yeah?"

"Can we not talk about this? I am so sick of talking about my friggin' back! Please. No more."

She sighs. "Okay. Do you want to go out somewhere?"

"Like where?"

"I don't know. We could go to the store, grab a pop or something."

"No. Maybe later, okay?"

She doesn't argue, this time. But as the weeks pass and I keep refusing, she pesters me more. I don't know why I don't want to go out. I just don't. I still have to go to rehab for physiotherapy three times a week, and that seems like enough. When I'm home, Mom does my exercises with me, but other than that, I'm free to play on the computer. I do that a lot, especially role-playing games.

They're perfect because in that little world on the screen, I'm not me.

Mom and Dad try to get me to go back to school, but I tell them I'm not ready, and they don't force the issue. It's already May and I say I'd rather go back in September. Start the new term fresh. They believe me.

I chat online sometimes too. Mrs. Green wanted our group to stay in touch. She said we should continue to support each other. It's weird, because the person I've stayed in contact with most is Jim the Jerk. Ever since the day we agreed on not caring what anyone else thinks, I figured at least he was honest. I don't have to pretend with him. I can say life sucks, and he doesn't start blabbing about how "normal" it can be for us. I can say I hate my life, and he understands. So when he says he wants to come by one day to show me his new van, I say, whatever, come over.

Jim's van has hand controls, and he's smug about driving it. When I ask why he didn't lose his license for drunk driving, he shrugs. "I guess they figured I suffered enough. Felt sorry for me, becoming a freak. Something like that. I only got a six-month suspension."

We drive around for about twenty minutes, and then he asks, "Anyone home at your place?"

"Why?"

"'Cause I'm due for a pee, but I'm not into a 'meet the family' scene."

"Nobody's home," I say. I don't add that's the only reason I got out without a family scene. Mom probably would have said she had to come along for the ride if she'd met Jim. He's scrawny, has a habit of sniffling, and his bloodshot eyes never quite meet anyone else's.

We drive back and go inside. Jim has started twitching by the time he gets to the bathroom, and I'm reminded of Will. When he was younger, it was always obvious when nature was calling. He'd hold on to his crotch and hop from one foot to the other. Then I start wondering how much sensation Jim has down there. Seems like a fair bit. By the time he comes out of the bathroom, he's calmer. He's even smiling.

"Feel better?" I ask.

"Oh, yeah," he says. "Way better. Fantastic."

"Wow. Never knew a trip to the can could be so amazing."

He laughs. "Well, it depends on what you do in the can."

"Right," I say. "I don't need to hear about it."

"Maybe you do." He hesitates, and then he pulls something out of his pocket. "I'm feeling generous. I could share."

Spiral

He opens his hand, and there's this little plastic bag of powder. White powder. He reaches into his pocket again and pulls out a short straw. "Voila," he says. "Care for a toot?"

I stare at the cocaine, and while part of my brain wants to say, *No, jerk, get out*, another voice inside me is saying, *Why not?*

Jim chuckles. "Trust me, it makes this crap life we're stuck with a whole lot easier to handle."

I don't know. I don't know. I don't know.

Jim is still smiling, his eyes are bright and he's looking straight at me. "The doctors dished out enough stuff for us in the beginning, but then they cut us off cold. We're supposed to be fine now, happy little campers tooling around on our butts. As if."

When I don't say anything, he moves to tuck the bag away. "Okay, that's cool. No biggie."

"Wait!" I blurt. "Maybe...just a little."

"Yeah," he says, "just a little." He moves next to me and shakes a small pile of powder out onto the arm of my chair. He takes out a slip of paper and uses the edge to carefully arrange the powder into a thin line. He hands me the straw.

I take it and place the end of the straw near a nostril.

"Better get that up the nose a bit more, girl. You don't want to waste any. And make sure you breathe in, not out. Don't want to blow it away."

I do as he says, and even though the voice inside is now screaming, *Stop, you idiot! Stop!* I bend over the powder and sniff it in. At first there's only a tingling in my nose. I rub it and look at Jim.

"Just give it a minute," he says.

And then..."Omigod," I breathe.

"Oh, yeah," Jim says. "What did I tell you?"

"Incredible," I say. And it is. I don't think I've ever felt so good. Ever, ever.

After about twenty minutes, Jim says, "Let's have a bit more." And we do. And it's beautiful.

Chapter Five

The coke high lasts for almost an hour. By the time it's over, Jim is gone, my mom is home and I feel like I'm at the bottom of a hole. The hole is deep, dirty, dark. I thought I was down before, but this is way worse.

I tell Mom I'm not hungry for dinner, I'm tired, going to bed early. I don't go straight to bed. I do a search on the Internet for information on cocaine. I already know some stuff about it. I've heard talk, and it was around sometimes, at parties. But I never even tried weed before. Why did I do this? I begin reading, and it's bad news. The words start blurring and I just shut the computer off, crawl into bed. It takes a long time to fall asleep, and for all that time I'm thinking how stupid I was. And how good it was. And that I want to do it again.

Jim messages me in the morning, and I ignore him. When he messages again later, when there's just me at home, slumped in my chair, trying to get into my online-game role, I reply. He comes over right away, and we work out a deal. I get regular payments from the government program. My parents have been banking most of the money, but they give some to me. I know they're hoping the money will entice me to go out with Lily, go to movies or out shopping. Since I haven't, a fair chunk of cash has piled up over the past few months.

"I don't want to do too much," I tell Jim. "Just a little, sometimes, when I need it."

"For sure," Jim says. "Gotta be smart about it."

Turns out that Jim has started dealing coke. He says it's cool to do his own thing, and he doesn't have to go to crap courses to train for a wheelchair-friendly job. "My supplier loves me. He figures my chair is a great cover."

I'm surprised at how much it costs, but then, I'll make it last. Just do a bit every day, or every other day, and if I ever want more, by then I'll have more money.

I do quite a bit right away. It is so freaking amazing! The next day, it's weird, but it seems like I need more just to get myself high. Within a few weeks, I need even more than that just to feel okay. When I'm not high, I feel like absolute crap. Worse than I've ever felt. Ever, ever.

But I can't stop. Mom is on my case all the time now, telling me I'm not eating enough, not doing my exercises regularly, my room is a mess, school will be starting in just a couple more months…

Lily still comes by, but not so much. She has a summer job and is putting in lots of hours. "I'm going to have enough saved for a car by the time I get my license," she says.

"Wow," I say. But I don't sound like I mean it.

She looks hurt, confused. "It'll be cool," she murmurs. "We'll go out for drives, okay, Abby? Just you and me."

"Yeah, that'll be real special," I say. And I roll my eyes. I regret that, instantly, but the damage is done.

"You know, Abby," Lily says, "maybe I liked you better when you were just pretending to be a cow. What's wrong with you?"

"I have a broken back, remember?"

"Right. And the whole world ends because of it? Is that it for you? Game over?"

"Oh, please," I sneer. "I don't need a corny pep talk. I hate myself, okay? Are you happy now I'm being honest? I'm a useless waste of space, Lily. End of story."

"God," she says. "I wish you wouldn't talk like that. I wish this never happened to you, Abby. So much. But since it has, I wish for you to be cured. I pray, every day, that they'll find some way to fix your spine. But until then, I wish…"

Spiral

"What?" I ask.

"I wish you would find a way to live again. You know, just have a life you enjoy. It can be done. Other people have carried on."

"I'm not other people."

"I know," she sighs. "I know."

She's quiet for a minute, and in the silence, I sniffle. "Do you have a cold again, Abby?" she asks.

I shrug. "I guess."

As soon as she leaves, I get my stuff out. I'm bent over the line, preparing to snort, when Will walks in.

"Abby, you want to…Hey! What's that? What are you doing?"

I try to cover the coke with my hand. "Nothing! What are *you* doing, barging in? Get out, you little brat!"

"I know what it is, Abby," he says quietly. "I'm not stupid." And then he races from my room, yelling at the top of his lungs, "Mom! Dad! Come quick!"

And they do. Will's voice is so frantic, they think maybe I've fallen or something. I'm still brushing the white dust off my chair, trying to stuff the bag back into my pocket, when they arrive.

Their faces. God, their faces are so awful. At first, there's fear. Then, when they see me sitting safely in my chair, there's relief. When they notice the details, when Will whispers, "Look. She's doing cocaine," their faces are utterly blank. For about ten seconds.

And then Mom is at me, pulling my hand from my pocket, snatching up the bag, holding it at arm's length, staring in horror. Dad's face flushes red, deep red. One hand forms a fist, and for one terrible second I think he's going to punch me. Instead his fist lands on the wall, and it leaves a hole.

"Is there more?" he asks.

Spiral

I shake my head.

"I'm going to tear every inch of this room apart, to check. Are you sure there's no more?"

I'm silent.

"Answer me!" he bellows.

"Maybe, a bit. In my dresser." I've never seen my father like this.

He strides over to the dresser and tips it. All the drawers crash forward, and, one by one, he empties them.

Mom is crying now, huge sobs, tears streaming down her face. She starts moaning, over and over, "So that's why. That's why. That's why."

"Mom?" I squeak.

"I should have known!" she says. "I should have seen! It's so bloody obvious now. I knew something was very wrong…Oh, Abby! How could you?"

Dad has found my stash, and he has it clutched in another fist. I notice it's

43

not the same hand he used to punch the wall, and when I look at that hand, I see that it's streaming blood.

"Dad! Your hand..."

"I don't give a damn about my hand, little girl. But this!" He raises the baggies high. "This!" And then he roars, "Is there more?"

"No! None. I swear."

"Where did you get it?" he shouts.

I don't answer.

He grabs my shoulder and shakes me.

Mom yelps, "Frank! Stop it!"

And he stops. He drops the bags and passes a hand over his face. Finally, he says, "I'm sorry, Abby." And then his shoulders start heaving up and down and he hunches over, and for the second time in my life, I'm watching my father cry.

Chapter Six

The next few weeks are the worst hell I've ever known. Worse even than the weeks after I broke my back. My parents get me admitted into a small treatment place out in the boonies. At first, I'm barely aware of my surroundings. There's just sickness and craving and craving and more soul-sucking craving. It's all I know, the need.

I slide into the pit. The pit is way deeper than the hole, darker, dirtier. I wish to be dead, to be done with all of it. If I could find a way, if I had even the tiniest bit of strength, I'd end it.

After that, there's nothing. Some part of me knows I exist, but no part of me cares that this is so. And then someone wheels my sorry ass outside, shoves me into a barn and parks me. I don't know how long it takes, but I start to notice things. Strange things. There's a certain smell. It's familiar. It wakens something.

And then there's a breath, on the top of my head. Something starts touching my hair, very softly. Tiny tingles race over my scalp, and slowly, I raise my hand. My hand is stroked, gently, steadily, by something warm and moist and soft. I open my eyes wide, tilt my head…and there's a horse. Its long brown nose is hanging over a stall door, and it's licking my hand.

"Oh!" I gasp. I yank my hand away, and the horse returns to nuzzling my head.

"Stop that," I say.

The horse lifts its nose and snorts. A fine, wet spray shoots out of its nostrils, and I'm showered in tiny drops. "Oh, gross. Thanks a lot!"

"Abby?" a voice asks. "Are you okay?"

I turn my head the other way and find Mrs. Green. "Uh. No. This horse just blew snot all over me."

She chuckles. "Yeah, I noticed. Charlie can be a pest sometimes."

"Charlie? That's his name?"

She nods.

I angle my head back toward the horse. "Hmph. Charlie."

His ears tip forward and his eyes take on a hopeful look.

"Right," says Mrs. Green. "Now he expects a treat. Want to give him one?" She rolls toward me and holds out a carrot.

I take the carrot and offer it to Charlie. His big head dips down and, very gently, he closes his lips around the carrot. Then he sucks the whole thing into his mouth and starts munching.

Mrs. Green doesn't say anything else and neither do I. I just watch Charlie eat the carrot. When he's done, he yawns, sighs and closes his eyes. His lower lip hangs loose. Black whiskers stand out around the end of his nose, and I reach up and touch one. Bad move. His nostrils twitch, he snorts and I'm sprayed again.

It's not gooey snot. It's more like being dampened by those spray bottles hair stylists use. I know this from the once upon a time in my life when I rode horses. Lily's cousin had some, and we spent our ten- and eleven-year-old summers riding. I wanted my own horse for years, but my parents couldn't afford one. Guess I outgrew the whole horse thing, because it's a long while since I've thought about it.

The next day, I'm rolled out to the barn again. And again, I'm left. I don't even see Mrs. Green around. I wonder what she was doing there anyway. It doesn't matter. It's not as if I want to talk to anyone. Charlie is perfect company. He eats his hay, and the steady munching sound is soothing. I focus on that sound, I breathe in his smell, that distinct horse odor, and for the first time in—how long?—I feel a whisper of peace. It's not a perfect peace. Maybe it's just the absence of desire.

When Charlie finishes his hay, he dozes for a while. Then he starts nuzzling my head again. "Okay, Charlie, enough already." I push myself away from his stall and turn to face him. This time, I'm out of range when he snorts.

"Hah," I say. "Missed me." I notice a small box of brushes placed on the floor outside his door. My gaze wanders to the door latch. It's set low, a simple bolt, out of his reach but easily within mine. There's a second hook, farther up but still within my grasp. I don't think about what I'm doing, I just do it. I roll forward, pick up the brushes, set them on my lap and open the door.

Charlie watches me. His ears prick forward and he lowers his head, but that's it. I edge into his stall, and he doesn't move. He's bigger than I thought he'd be, much bigger. The top of my head is barely higher than the bottom of his belly. "Hey," I whisper. "How's it going?"

Spiral

He stands perfectly still. I dip into the box and pull out a brush. My hand is shaking as I reach for him. "Good boy," I croon. "Here we go." I start brushing his leg. On the third stroke, my shaky grasp fumbles, and I drop the brush.

"Damn," I mutter. I start turning my chair so that I can pick it up, but Charlie gets to it first. He grabs the brush in his mouth, lifts it high in the air, wiggles his lips and drops it. It falls right into my lap.

"Wow," I laugh. "You're good."

When I take the brush again, I'm not so shaky. "I can do this," I tell him. And maybe he understands, because he lowers his head until we're face to face, and the invitation is clear.

"Ah. You want me to work on this part, do you?" I place the brush on the flat part of his forehead, between his eyes, and draw it down. Again and again. Then I go to work on his cheek, his neck, his chest. When that side is done, I place a hand on his head and push, hoping he'll get the idea to move over. He does.

"You're a smart boy, aren't you, Charlie?"

A voice from the door answers. "He sure *is* a smart boy. He's our School Master."

I spin around and find a young woman. She's in a wheelchair. She's smiling. "You must be our new working student. Abby, right? Pleased to meet you. I'm Taylor." She holds out a hand.

I take it and am surprised at how strong it feels. "Yeah," I say, "I'm Abby. But you must have me mixed up with someone else."

"Why do you say that?" she asks.

"Because I'm not working and I'm not a student."

She frowns. "Hmm. Didn't Mrs. Green explain it to you?"

Spiral

"Explain what?"

"I guess she didn't. Okay. It's simple. You are here to work. Don't worry, I'll teach you the routine. The work helps to pay for your room and board, and it also pays for your lessons." She grins. "No free rides here."

"What's that supposed to mean?"

"Sorry," she says. "Stupid inside joke. No free rides, as in, your riding lessons aren't free."

I stare at her. "Are you nuts? I'm not here to take riding lessons."

"You're not? I heard you like horses."

"Uh. Wheelchair? Paralyzed? Get it?"

She says, "No."

"What?"

The smile is back. "In case you missed it, I'm a paraplegic too, and I ride almost every day."

"Yeah? Well, good for you. That doesn't mean…"

Taylor cuts me off. "Charlie will get you started. He's the best School Master I've ever met, very patient and gentle, and he really knows his stuff."

I hold up a hand. "You're wasting your breath. I'm not riding. But what's the deal with calling a horse a School Master?"

Taylor's head tips to one side, and she regards me narrowly. "A School Master is a horse who has done so much advanced training he knows more about riding than some people who've been riding for years."

I shake my head.

"Don't believe me?" Taylor asks. "Too bad. Since you're not going to ride, you won't find out if I'm right." She shrugs. "Your loss. But you still have to work."

"Why? I thought I was here to… recover. And I did. So now I think I'll just go home."

"Have you talked to Dr. Scott about that?" she asks.

I don't answer her. I've heard that name, Dr. Scott, but it isn't anyone connected to me, is it? I need to talk to my parents. My parents. I haven't talked to them since I came here. Not once. It's as if they've written me off.

Chapter Seven

When I get back to the house, for the first time I take a careful look around. It's a small house, nothing fancy. There are a few rooms, but most of the doors are closed. I know there are other people here. One woman has brought me food, changed my sheets, washed me and forced my legs through the exercises. I don't even know her name. I figure she's some sort of nurse.

I search my memory and find vague images of other people being around, but I was too out of it to care. For one awful moment, I wonder if they're creepers, people who intend to sell me into slavery or use me for spare body parts. But then, my parents did bring me here. I remember that.

"Hello?" I call. "Hello?"

It takes a few minutes, but at last I hear the sound of footsteps approaching. The steps move steadily, clunk, clunk, clunk. I've parked myself in the living room or whatever it is, the room with mismatched chairs and an old tiny TV. I wait there, holding my breath.

"Abby?" a voice calls. "Is that you?"

"In here," I croak.

A slender woman wearing khakis and a T-shirt walks into the room.

Her dark hair is swept up in a bun, and a pair of wire-rimmed glasses perch on her nose. She smiles. "Good to have you back in the land of the living. How are you?"

"I want to call my parents. I'm going home."

She sinks into a chair and peers at me. "I'm afraid that's not possible."

I stare at her. "What do you mean, not possible?"

She says, "Just how it sounds. Your parents have signed you in for a minimum six-month program, and for now, I'm responsible for your care."

"Is that right?" I say. "And if you don't mind my asking, who the hell are you?"

"I'm Dr. Scott."

"I want to call them. Right now. Where's the phone?"

"There is no phone available for patients," she says quietly. "I'm in constant contact with your parents, Abby. And while they miss you very much and would love to talk to you, they understand that's not how we work here."

"You're kidding, right? I can't call my parents? My friends?"

"No phone calls. You can, however, write them a letter. And there are a few letters here for you. Until now, you showed no interest in them. They're in your bedside table."

I want to rush to my room and find my letters. I have a sudden desperate need for my mom, my dad, for Will. For Lily. For Jim. This last thought startles me, and instantly I know it's not Jim I want. It's the coke. The lovely, beautiful, horrible coke. A tremor runs through me, vibrates right down to my bones.

"I want to go home!" I scream.

"You will," she says quietly. "When you're ready."

"I'm ready now!"

"No, you're not. Far from it. But if it's any comfort, you're much closer to going home now than you were two days ago."

"What do you know about it? You haven't even talked to me until now. No counseling. No amazing words of wisdom. What kind of doctor are you, anyway?"

She raises her brows. "I'm a psychiatrist. But while I'm here to oversee your treatment, Abby, I'm not in charge of it."

"Who is?"

"You are." She pauses, watches my reaction and then adds, "You'll have help, of course."

"Really? Who's going to help me?"

She smiles. "There's myself. I run Spiral. That's what our place is called. We offer equine-assisted therapy for treatment of various problems. Most of our clients come to us three times per week. We only have space for one resident at this time."

"That would be me?" I ask.

"Yes. There's also our wonderful housekeeper and nurse, Hilda. There's Taylor, who will instruct you on the work. Mrs. Green may visit sometimes. And then there's your teacher."

"My teacher?"

"Of course. You've met him, and he's already done a great deal for you. Charlie made contact."

I blink a few times before I answer. "Um. Charlie's a horse. And you're saying he made contact? Like he's some sort of alien?"

Dr. Scott laughs. "Well, in a way, horses *are* aliens. At least in the sense that their minds are so different from ours. The basic difference is that they're prey animals while we are predators."

"Maybe *you're* a predator, but I'm not."

"Ah, but you are. Humans are designed to be hunters. Our eyes are set on the front of our heads, like wolves and lions, not to the side like deer and horses. Many of us eat meat. We have a few pointy, canine teeth. And the way we think…it's predatory too. I'm not saying we think about actual hunting, but we do tend to think in straight lines. We set goals and aim for them, as if we're aiming arrows at a target." She shrugs. "That's how we've evolved."

I can't argue with this, but I don't want to agree with her either. "Not everyone sets goals. Some people have nothing to aim for."

"True. But that doesn't stop them from being predators. There are some things we can't change. However, it is possible for us to learn some of the ways of prey animals. We can't *be* them, but we can observe and learn."

"Learn what?" I ask. "How to run away?" As I say this, I realize it's an excellent idea. Run away.

She shrugs. "There's that. But I find the most valuable quality they teach is awareness. They are aware of their surroundings in ways we seldom are. They are in tune, always, with their senses. Smell, sight, taste, touch, sound. Most of us have those senses too, but prey animals tend to use the information differently. They cast a net of awareness around themselves. And then they extend this to those in their herd. They seldom choose to isolate themselves. And because they hold awareness in a circular manner, they also think in a circular manner."

"Thinking in circles? That doesn't sound too smart."

"No? Why not? If the straight line doesn't work, if the thing directly ahead doesn't interest you, why not look around instead? Why not take some curves?"

There's the shrink in her, showing itself. Before I can say anything, she adds, "But I'm talking too much. It's better if Charlie shows you."

Charlie. He's the only one around here I'm going to miss. I say, "I want to go read my letters now."

Chapter Eight

There are several letters from Mom and Dad. What Dr. Scott told me was true. They did sign me in here for a minimum of six months. I find a calendar on my wall and figure out I've been here for one month. Five to go? As if.

Mom and Dad say they love me, miss me, but feel Spiral is my best chance to recover. Mom writes: *Mrs. Green recommended this program for you after she heard that you liked horses. I told her the name of the place put me off because it made me think of a downward spiral. She said to think of it like this: spirals circle inward, not down. They can also lead you out.*

Will has written too. His letter isn't long, but it's honest. He says: *I'm not sorry I ratted you out, Abby. You were getting really mean, you know. And I want my big sister back, not the druggie freak.*

The druggie freak. He doesn't say anything about the cripple freak. He doesn't care about that? I try to get angry over this, that he doesn't even see that problem. Instead I cry because he doesn't see it.

And then there's a letter from Lily. *I wish you'd trusted me enough to*

Spiral

tell me, Abby. That's what hurts the most, you know? I always thought we could tell each other anything. How would you feel if I got into that garbage and hid it from you? Would you feel betrayed? Never mind. I don't want to make you feel guilty, I just want the old Abby back, the sweet fun person I've always known. Do you really think I loved you for your body? Ha ha! Get on with it, girl! Stop feeling sorry for yourself. There, I said it. And if friends can't tell each other the truth, who can? Please get well soon. Write soon! I miss you.

I am aching to see them. I have to see them. There are no locks on the doors at Spiral, nothing to stop me from leaving. I hunt around in my room for money and don't find a cent. Not one cent, never mind the quarter I hoped for. If I could just wheel myself to the main road, I'm sure I could find a pay phone. Or hitch a ride to one. Then I could call home, and Mom and Dad would pick me up. For sure they would. I'll tell them I hate it here, I'm better, I'll never do coke again. I'll go to school.

But I don't have a quarter. So I'll get to the road and I'll hitch a ride all the way. That's actually better. I can tell them in person, and once I'm there, they won't send me back.

I wait until dark, until after Hilda has done her check on me, and then I haul myself out of bed. I'm already tired, but that's not going to stop me. I'll make it. I put a pair of rain pants over my jeans, and once I've got my jacket on, I'm ready. I can't carry all my other stuff, but I'm sure we can pick it up later. I take the letters, though. I tuck them in alongside my butt and ease open the door to my room. I peer into the hall and see no one, hear nothing. I roll along the hall, get to the front door, open it. And then I'm outside and pushing with all my might. The faster I can get away, the better my chances.

I'm gone maybe two minutes when Hilda appears, jogging at my side. She talks into a cell phone. "First shift," she says. And that's all.

I'm furious. The fury gives me energy I didn't know I had. So, fine, she can follow me. Who cares? She's not stopping me, not unless she grabs my chair and forces me around, and I'll fight her every inch. But she doesn't try to stop me, and she doesn't talk. I ignore her and push on.

I'd forgotten how long the driveway is, but when I finally make the road, I'm elated. I did it! Only now, when I see the road stretching out in both directions, a straight line, I hesitate. Which way? I'm not sure. The road is dark, no streetlights, no headlights from cars. Well, it's got to be just a matter of time before a car comes along. I think maybe Dad made a right turn into the driveway when we came, so I cross the road and head to the left. Hilda keeps following.

"Go to hell," I yell at her.

She says nothing. I can't stand the thought of sitting here, waiting for someone to pick me up, so I keep going. We go for a long while, maybe an hour, and my arms are burning. If I had some coke, I'd hardly notice. I'd be stronger. I need some. Really, really need some. *Now.* I put my head down and keep going.

By the time the lights of a car come up behind us, I could weep with relief. I turn to the side and stick out my thumb. The car stops, but its headlights are blinding, and I can't see the driver. Are they going to pick me up?

Spiral

Then Hilda is walking toward the car, and I hear her talking to someone.

"Don't listen to her!" I yell. "She's a psycho! Please, help me!"

And then, unbelievably, I see Hilda climb into the car. Or maybe it's a van? It is a van, because the side door slides open, a ramp descends and a wheelchair rolls out onto the pavement.

"Second shift," the person in the chair says. It's Taylor.

"Oh my God!" I scream. And I start rolling again. She catches up to me easily, and, like Hilda, she keeps pace behind me. Says nothing.

I start to cry. The tears roll silently down my cheeks, snot streams out of my nose. But I don't quit. Another car will come. I'll wheel myself out into the middle of the road, and if it doesn't stop, if it just drives right over me, I won't care. I won't.

But another car doesn't come. There's just Taylor and me, rolling along the pavement on a dark road that looks like it goes straight on forever. And I can't go on forever. I stop.

Taylor pulls up beside me. "Just breathe," she says.

And I do. I just breathe. And when I've caught enough breath, she leans forward and gently wipes my face with a tissue. There's not enough strength left in my arms to push her away.

Softly, she says, "You've got stamina, Abby, I'll give you that."

"Why don't you just leave me alone?"

She shakes her head. "You're running, right? Going for safety. We get that. And we won't stop you. But we won't let you go alone, Abby. You need companions for the road."

"You're going to follow me all the way home?"

"If we must, we will. The third shift will arrive soon."

The third shift. I get it. They take turns. "Why don't you just give me a ride, then?"

She shrugs. "We can't. It's not part of our commitment to you and your family."

"So if I actually make it home, then what?"

"I don't know for sure. It's likely your parents will bring you back here. That's part of the agreement too."

I slump down in my chair. I'm done. Beat.

Taylor waits. Finally, she says, "When the van comes, Abby, you can go back to Spiral with me. Your choice."

"No!" I say. "I have no choices here! I'm a prisoner."

"I don't think so," she says. "I think you *were* a prisoner. You were chained to a drug. Even now, you might let it snare you again. You might choose that."

"And what if I did?" I glare at her. "At least it would be my choice!"

"Is that what you want, Abby?" Her eyes find mine and hold them. There is no blame in her gaze. There's just the question.

"No," I whisper. "That's not what I want. I don't know what it is I want, but it's not that."

"The beast still wants it though. Doesn't it? The thing inside you craves it. It's part of us, that beast voice. It's the one that demands food and sleep, the basic needs. When your body forms an addiction, the beast says it needs the drug now too. You hear: *I'm hungry. I'm tired. I need a hit.* When you hear that, you must change it. Say, No, *It* needs a hit, not me."

"How do you know about It?" I ask.

"Been there. Done that," she says.

When the van pulls up behind us, I get in with Taylor.

Chapter Nine

They give me the next day off, and I spend the first half sleeping. By afternoon, I feel restless and decide to visit Charlie. There are several cars parked in front of the barn today, and inside I find a number of people. There's a kid wearing leg braces and a woman with a cane. One little girl looks perfectly fine physically, but her eyes are empty. It's like she's simply not there.

I don't speak to any of them, but when I find Charlie's stall vacant, I roll all the way down the aisle to the end of the barn. There I discover a covered riding arena. Charlie is trotting about, carrying a boy. If the boy smiled any bigger, his face would break in two.

Taylor is parked in the center of the arena, watching the pair closely. "Awesome, kiddo!" she calls. And while it didn't seem possible, the boy's smile widens.

I notice a small alcove in the arena wall, just a short distance from the entryway, and head for that. I park myself there and keep watching. A few minutes later, the woman who had the cane comes in, mounted on a plump gray mare. Dr. Scott walks on the far side of the horse, and a man walks on the near side. I can see that he's holding the woman's leg, plus a strap attached to her waist. He's helping her stay in the saddle. It looks like a tough job. But after a few minutes, I can see that the rider is getting better at keeping her balance.

"Good stuff," the man says. "Can you feel that? How the movement of the horse is making your hips and legs work as if you're walking?"

I don't hear her reply because what he said stuns me. Being on a horse is like walking?

He goes on. "It's one of the best therapies we have for MS. If you can ride regularly, you might be able to put that cane away for a while yet."

Wow. Riding can even…No. Maybe it can do something for MS, like delay its effect. But for me? No. The doctors were quite clear that my chances for recovery are almost zero.

Before long, the boy on Charlie is finished his lesson, and so is the woman. I think maybe that's it, but as they leave the arena, the empty girl comes in. A woman has her by the hand, and in her other hand, she holds a pony's lead line. She murmurs to the girl, but I can't see any reaction. Then Dr. Scott comes in. She murmurs too, and together, she and the woman lift the little girl up onto the pony's back. Now the girl reacts. She draws her legs up, puts her head on her knees and wraps her arms around them. She's curled herself into a ball.

The pony stands patiently, and so do Dr. Scott and the woman. I feel like I'm spying, like I shouldn't be there. But Dr. Scott glances my way and gives me a quick smile. She holds a finger to her lips, and I decide to stay put.

Minutes pass and nothing else happens. Then the pony does

something strange. He bends his neck until he can reach the girl's leg with his nose. He starts sniffing, and then his lips begin to wiggle.

A small sound escapes from the girl, and the pony stops. But that leg slides down. And then the other leg slides down. The girl is still hunched over, but at least she's not in a ball anymore. Her arms are wrapped around the pony's neck now, her face pressed into his mane.

The pony takes a small step. I didn't see the woman with the lead rope ask him to do this, but she doesn't stop him either. He takes another small step. Another. And that's it.

Dr. Scott rubs the pony's neck. "All right, Sugar. Thank you. I think that's enough for today."

Together, she and the woman lift the girl down from Sugar's back. They move to leave, but the girl's arms are still wrapped around Sugar's neck. She's clinging to him like she'll never let go. Then Sugar swings his head round again, circling her small body within the curve of his neck. I can't believe what I'm seeing. It's as if he's returning her hug.

Once again, the women wait. Finally Sugar straightens his neck, and only then does the girl release him. The woman takes the girl's hand once more, and without a word, they all walk out.

Chapter Ten

"You've got to be kidding!" I'm in the barn with Taylor. It's 8:00 AM, and she just finished telling me I'm expected to muck out five horse stalls.

"Not kidding," she says cheerfully. "Allow me to demonstrate." And she does. She grabs hold of a wheelbarrow, one of those square plastic ones with

Spiral

a handle straight across the back. Then she picks up a manure fork and drops it into the wheelbarrow. She keeps her grip on the barrow with one hand and uses the other to push her chair into an empty stall.

"Pay attention," she says. "This is a lot like rocket science."

"Yeah, right," I mutter. But I'm watching.

Taylor slides the fork under a pile of manure, lifts it and gives it a little shake. Wood shavings are used to "bed" the stalls, and when Taylor shakes the fork, the shavings sift out. She's left with a scoop of mostly poop, and she lifts her arms high, turns and drops it into the barrow. "There! Did you see that?"

I give her an eye roll.

"As for the wet spots, you want to get those too." She deftly scoops a patch of soggy shavings, dumps it into the barrow and then offers me the fork. "Your turn," she says.

Taylor made it look easy. I manage to get the fork under a pile, but when I give it a shake, half the poop falls off. Then I fumble the turn and drop even more. Instead of one neat pile of poop to scoop, now I've got scattered lumps. I give Taylor a look.

She shrugs. "Takes some practice. Don't worry, there's a steady supply. Oh, and when the wheelbarrow is full, you just haul it down to the far door and dump it in the pit there."

"It's going to take me until tomorrow to do five stalls," I whine.

She shakes her head. "Can't take that long. You need to be done before the horses come back in from pasture. Don't worry. Five stalls is nothing. I once worked at a place where I did twenty, every day."

Spiral

My jaw drops. "Twenty?"

"Yup. It was tough." She pulls up a sleeve and flexes her arm muscles. "You didn't think I got this buff just from wheeling my chair, did you?"

"I never thought about it," I say. This is true. It's also true that Taylor is one of the fittest people I've ever seen.

"Riding helps too," she says. "It's the best exercise there is to build core body strength."

"Yeah, yeah," I mutter. But when she leaves to do some other chores, I go after the manure with some serious energy. I wouldn't mind looking as good as her.

I'm dripping sweat by the time I'm done. Dr. Scott comes by with a water bottle. "Looks like you could use this," she says.

I take it and guzzle half the water. "Thanks."

"You're welcome." She glances around clean stall number five and says, "Nice job. I'd say you deserve lunch."

Right on cue, my stomach rumbles. I send her a sheepish look. "I guess it's time."

"Come on. I'll walk back to the house with you, and we can clean up."

She adjusts her stride to match my chair, and we're halfway there when I blurt, "What's wrong with that little girl?"

Dr. Scott halts and turns to face me. Her gaze is troubled, and she places a hand on my shoulder. "That was really something with Sugar yesterday, wasn't it?"

I nod.

She sighs. "I can't tell you what happened to her. We feel it's important to respect the privacy of our clients. But I can tell you this. She was attacked. Her physical wounds have long since healed, but the psychological wounds…no. She became catatonic. That is, she withdrew completely into herself. She doesn't speak, nor does she show any sign that she hears what others say. All therapy that's been attempted has failed to reach her."

"My god. That's horrible!"

"It is. But what you saw, with Sugar…" A smile tugs at the corners of her mouth.

"He did it, didn't he? He reached her. I saw it!" I'm smiling now too. Sugar, the alien, made contact.

"It was a start," Dr. Scott says. "We were delighted with what happened. It's too early to know if it's going to work, but we're hopeful."

"So she's coming back?"

"Yes. She's scheduled to come three times a week. After a few weeks, we should know if equine-assisted therapy can help her."

"What's her name?" I ask.

Dr. Scott hesitates. "How about this? Let's wait and see if she can tell you that herself some day. Then I'll know we succeeded."

"Are you saying I should talk to her?"

"Maybe not just yet, but you're certainly welcome to observe her sessions. Then if a time comes when it feels right, yes, by all means—speak to her."

I spend the first half of the afternoon watching the riding lessons. The girl doesn't come, but it's okay watching the others for a while. I spend the second half of the afternoon with Charlie. I get permission from Taylor to take him out on a lead line, and we head for the nearest patch of grass. Charlie seems entirely content to graze, and I'm content to watch him. He munches steadily, gradually circling around my chair.

The October sun is warm, and it feels great on my aching shoulders. I relax, soak in the sun, soak in Charlie. He too looks relaxed, really into the grass, but I begin to notice he's not exactly out of it. His ears are constantly flicking, back and forth. When a door at the house closes, his ears tilt in that direction. When another horse in the barn nickers, he lifts his head and nickers back. When a breeze rustles through a nearby shrub, he pauses and turns to look. His nostrils widen as he sniffs the air. I feel as though I could fall asleep here, and I'd be safe with Charlie on guard.

My eyelids droop. I drift. Out of nowhere, everywhere, I hear, "*I need a toot. Now.*"

The beast isn't sleeping. "*It* needs a toot," I say fiercely. "*It* wants one. Not me. Not Abby. Never again. *Never.*"

The beast slithers away, growling. My eyes refocus, and I find Charlie staring at me. "Sorry," I mutter. "Cave lion attack."

He snorts softly and returns to grazing. I drift again. When I awake, I find Charlie's head hanging over my shoulder, his big nose resting in my lap. I lean my cheek on his and wish I could stay, just here, forever.

Chapter Eleven

"Wow," Taylor says. "You're done in half the time it took you yesterday."

"Practice makes perfect," I answer smugly.

"Yeah, for sure. That's great. Now you can help me spread fresh bedding."

I give her a look. "That's my reward?"

"Yup," she says. "Because if we get finished early enough, we'll have time for your lesson."

"Excuse me? My lesson?"

She tips her head to one side. "Abby, you've spent enough time watching. That's almost all you do, watch. Don't you think it's time for some action?"

"Cleaning stalls is action," I say.

She bursts out laughing. "Girl, your idea of action is pretty bad. Cleaning stalls is work. Dirty work. But action! Well, let's see. We could take a poll on that. I know some people who have all sorts of ideas. Take my boyfriend, for example. Wait. That came out wrong. I don't want you to take my boyfriend…"

I interrupt. "You have a boyfriend?"

"Darn right I have a boyfriend. And you can't have him."

"I don't want your boyfriend, you idiot. I'm just sort of…"

"What?" she asks. "Surprised? In case you hadn't noticed, I am one hot babe."

"Oh, man," I laugh. "Not conceited much, are you?"

"Not much," she says. "Now let's get back to the point. Your riding lesson. Today."

I stall for time. "What does he look like? Is he cute?"

"Uh-uh," she says. "Not falling for it. Although, I will make you a deal. If you do well at your lesson, I'll show you his picture."

"Oooh. His picture."

"Abby. Do we have a deal?"

"Fine. I'll get on a horse." I try to hide the thrill of excitement those words create, but Taylor doesn't miss a thing.

"All right," she grins. "That's what I like to see."

The whole time we're spreading fresh wood shavings in the stalls,

I slide between excitement and fear. What if I fall off? It won't be the same as it was. I won't feel the horse under me. It's a stupid idea. I never should have got sucked into this. I can't wait to get on.

When Taylor says, "Okay, let's get Charlie," I'm tempted to back out. I can't do this. And then I hear It. *"We need coke. Then we'll be fine."*

"Shut up!" I say.

Taylor looks at me, eyes wide with surprise. Then she sighs. "Atta girl, Abby. Come on. Grooming Charlie will help."

I do battle with the beast as I wait for her to lead Charlie between a pair of ramps. There's a square platform at the top of each ramp, and she tells me to work from one side while she does the other. I wheel up onto the platform, and for the first time I can see the top of Charlie's back. I run a hand along his spine, his strong, perfect spine. And the beast fades.

As I work the brush over Charlie's coat, it's as though his large warm body absorbs all my jitters. I don't understand how it works, but by the time we're done, I'm calm.

Taylor places the saddle on Charlie's back and attaches the girth on her side. Then she passes the girth under Charlie's belly and asks me to grab hold of it from my side. I pull it snug and buckle it.

"We make quite a team," she says. "Now put on that hard hat there and climb aboard!"

Dr. Scott arrives just as I finish strapping on the helmet. "All set, Abby? I'll be your side walker today. I think you have enough strength that we'll be okay without someone holding the other side too."

"You think?" I ask.

"Yes. But if it turns out I'm wrong, don't worry. We'll stop right away."

I take a deep breath. I rub Charlie's neck. It should be easy. I'm quite the expert at moving myself from my chair to the toilet. This isn't so different. I lean forward and grasp the saddle, placing one hand on each side.

"That's right, Abby," Taylor says. "Just transfer over and sit sideways to start."

I go for it. And I'm on Charlie's back!

"Excellent," she says. "Now, we can help swing your leg over, but you might want to try it yourself first."

Dr. Scott is standing on Charlie's far side. "I'm here. Ready when you are."

Another deep breath. Then I take hold of my right leg, pick it up and haul it over Charlie's neck. I drop it, and for one awful second I think the rest of me is going to follow my leg. But I get a handful of Charlie's mane and steady myself.

"Good job," says Taylor. "Now take a minute to get comfortable. See if you can straighten up a bit."

I realize that I'm hunched over. I brace my hands on the front of the saddle and push my torso upright. I wobble. Man, Charlie hasn't even moved yet and I'm having trouble.

Chapter Twelve

"Just relax, Abby," Taylor says. "Take a moment to be aware of your body. Your head. Your neck. Your shoulders." Taylor's voice is soft and low. "Keep moving down. Be aware of your back. Your arms. Your chest. Your belly. Take a breath and let it fill your belly. Exhale."

"This is like the yoga exercises I've done," I say.

Taylor nods. "Yes, it is. Let's keep going. Be aware of your bum."

I giggle.

"None of that," she says sternly. But her eyes are laughing. "All right. Now your thighs. I know you have limited sensation, but some is better than nothing. Try to connect with it. Move along to your knees. Your calves. Your feet. Another breath. Fill your belly. Hold it. Exhale."

She pauses and looks at me. "How are you doing?"

I realize that much of the tension I felt has gone. "Good," I say.

"All right. Now, where your body connects with Charlie's, be aware of that. Let me know when you feel you've found him."

Of course I see Charlie, his black mane flowing in front of me, his ears. I look down and find his shoulders. Then I find him with my hands, I stroke his neck. I can smell him. I feel removed from him where my butt sits on the saddle, but if I go further...There's warmth. His body heat warms my legs. And there's the faintest sensation of pressure where my calves rest against his sides.

I smile at Taylor. "I've got him."

"Excellent. Let's move." She takes hold of Charlie's lead line and starts walking. He follows. I stay with Charlie.

Dr. Scott takes hold of my thigh and calf and keeps pace beside us. "Okay?" she asks.

"Yes!"

When we enter the arena, nobody speaks. We just move as one, a tiny herd of three. I'm astonished to feel a faint motion in my hips, something I haven't felt for so long...The joint is sliding up and down, as if I really am walking. I barely notice when Dr. Scott lets go. She stays at our side, but I feel a rush of freedom when I realize she's no longer holding on. It's the way I felt when Dad taught me to ride a bike and there was that moment when he let go.

"Can I have the lead line?" I ask.

Taylor grins. "Feeling that confident, Abby?"

"For sure. Please, just for a minute. I trust Charlie."

"Okay." She stops, Charlie stops and she hands me the line. "You'll be okay to steer with just this for now. We can put the bridle on for next time." She steps back.

"Um," I say. "How do I make him go?"

"Ah! Allow me to begin the lesson. Try not to think of it as *making* him go. Think of it as *asking*. Ask him."

"There's a difference?"

"Yes," she says. "There is. It's an attitude more than anything. Making a horse do something implies the use of force. *Asking* is done between partners."

"Okay. I like that. Partners. So how do I ask?"

"Do you recall when I told you that Charlie is a School Master?"

I nod.

"If you were to squeeze with your calves, that pressure would tell him to go forward, right?"

I give her a look.

"But," she says, "it will take some time before you can do that. Chances are you'll never be able to manage that. So you need a tool."

"Allow me," says Dr. Scott. She jogs out of the arena and returns a moment later carrying two whips. They're about as long as my leg, with tufts on one end and handles on the other. Dr. Scott gives one to me.

"Notice it has a loop near the handle?" Taylor asks. "Slip that over your wrist and hold the handle in your hand. I think one will do for now."

I do as she says and find my hands full. I have a lead rope in one hand, a whip in the other and no way to hold on to Charlie's mane or the saddle.

"We really shouldn't be doing this much on your first lesson," Taylor says. "Are you sure you're solid enough up there, Abby?"

I hesitate. Then I nod firmly. "I just want to try."

"Fine. Now I want you to use the whip as if it were your leg. Just lay it along beside your leg and give Charlie a light tap. He'll understand what you're asking. And one more thing. If you want to stop, you need to be able to shift your weight back. Just tip your center enough that Charlie can feel it. Can you do that?"

I give it a try, and while there's a second when I'm afraid I'll tip too far, I manage it.

"All right. Whenever you're ready."

I gather myself, and then carefully, gently, I move the whip. Nothing happens.

"You're tapping your boot, Abby. Move the whip farther back."

I glance down and see that she's right. I position the whip again.

"Look up and forward," Taylor says. "Focus your thoughts. Charlie feels that too."

I look up. Forward. I tap. And Charlie starts walking. I'm flooded with sensation, so much that I can barely catch one before another one hits. A lurch of fear in the pit of my stomach. Confusion over controlling my body. Then, rising and swelling, there's joy. Amazed, giddy joy!

We walk all the way to the end of the arena. I tug lightly on Charlie's lead line, and he curves into a turn. I feel myself start to slide. But before I go too far, Charlie pushes out with his shoulder, brings himself fully under me. And we keep going, back the other way.

I come to a halt in front of Taylor and Dr. Scott. I look down at them, and their smiles are huge.

"How do you feel, Abby?" Dr. Scott asks.

I grin. "Tall," I say. "I feel tall."

Chapter Thirteen

The next few days pass in a haze so thick I can't tell if I'm happy or crazy. Something broke loose inside me when I rode Charlie, and it's floating just beyond my reach. Before this, I thought I was getting better. I wasn't so angry. I was trying. I was almost okay.

But while the ride was wonderful, there's still an ache. My back is still broken. And I'm a terrible person, because I find myself thinking if only I could ride properly, it would be so much easier. That greed makes me feel guilty. Then it reminds me of the horrible guilt I feel about my parents.

They gave up so much for me. My dad's car. My mom's garden. So much more. And I was so awful to them in return. It seems finding me doing cocaine was the worst for them. Then I wonder how much it's costing to keep me here. How can I ever make this right?

I keep this to myself. I know Taylor and Dr. Scott suspect something, but they don't ask and I don't tell. What good would it do to talk about it? I throw myself into the work, feeding the horses, cleaning, filling water buckets. I hang out with Charlie when I can. And I watch for the little girl.

Somehow, I've come to believe that if she can get better, I can too. I want to help her. I want to put my arms around her and make all the pain go away. I don't want to think about what happened to make her the way she is. It must have been very bad, very ugly. Maybe uglier than what lives inside me.

It is still there. Maybe It will be around for the rest of my life. I wish I'd never wakened that creature. Never fed it, never let it out of its cave. It's like a recurring nightmare, something that leaps out and scares me breathless, but there's no way to erase it.

I've seen things in my life, like when I was nine and this bully at school punched another kid so hard his lip split wide open. Teeth and blood poured out and he screamed. That sickened me, and I could never get the image out of my head. I used to wish so hard I hadn't seen that. Those ugly things we witness, the ugly we find in ourselves…Maybe they must exist so when we find the good, we can be grateful for it.

And maybe that's why I'm obsessed with the little girl. When she comes again, I watch from the alcove. It starts out as a repeat of the first time. The silence. Curling into a ball. Sugar nudging her leg until she sits astride. It all goes faster this time, and I watch closely. Will she speak? Will she hear? I want to do something, talk to her.

Talk to her. Right. I don't see the point in talking. Why should she?

I keep watching. When they lift her off Sugar's back, she clings to him again. Once more, he curves his neck in a hug. This is an image I want to hold in my head. This.

But when Sugar lets go, she doesn't accept it. The most primitive, shrill, hair-raising scream bursts from her tiny frame. And then she's raining blows on Sugar's neck. She's hitting him, again and again and again.

A shudder runs through Sugar's white body, and Dr. Scott puts herself between the girl and the pony. "No!" she says sharply. "You can't hurt him. Hit me if you must, but not Sugar."

As suddenly as it started, the assault stops. The girl stands, shaking, gasping. Dr. Scott moves to put an arm around her, and her small frame stiffens. Everything freezes.

And then Sugar pushes toward her. He puts his little nose square in her chest and shoves. It isn't a hard shove, but it moves her backward. He steps toward her again, but as Dr. Scott goes to grab his halter, he licks the girl's face. Once, twice. Then he lowers his head and stands quietly.

The girl reaches for his cheek. She strokes him. She says, clearly, "I'm sorry, Sugar."

Spiral

Sugar lifts his head into the girl's hand and closes his eyes as she continues to rub him.

"Ah," says Dr. Scott. "There you go. Sugar forgives you."

Is it that easy? Really? I let out a breath I didn't know I was holding.

"I love Sugar," the girl says.

"So do I," says Dr. Scott. "So do I."

Chapter Fourteen

A week passes. And another. And another. I work. I ride Charlie, and every time it gets better. I meet Taylor's boyfriend, and he is the sweetest guy. He plainly adores Taylor, and after he's gone, I ask her if she's going to marry him. She says maybe, but not yet. She's happy with things as they are.

Spiral

I watch the little girl ride Sugar. It's like watching a tightly curled flower bud opening to the sun. The blossoming is slow, but I can see it happening, petal by petal. She speaks. She sits upright on Sugar. She looks around. Her eyes hold growing light.

I'm hanging out with Charlie one day, just sitting outside his stall in that place where he made contact. It's a safe place to think. When he nuzzles my head, I reach up and pat him. "You're such a good guy, Charlie, you know that?"

"Is he as good as Sugar?" a small voice asks.

I turn my chair, and there she is. The girl. "Yes," I say. "He's as good as Sugar. He's helping me get better."

She nods. "Sugar helped me too. He never asked me anything. He just liked me."

"Yeah, I know what you mean."

"Sugar understands a lot," she says.

I smile. "Horses are pretty special that way."

"Sugar's not a horse. He's a pony." She tilts her head to one side. "What's wrong with you, anyway? You look okay to me."

"Oh," I say, "I'm almost better."

"Good," she says. "Are you going to watch me ride again today?"

"I wouldn't miss it."

"All right then. Come on. Hurry up. Sugar needs his apple." She races off, her dark ponytail flying behind her.

"Wait up," I call.

She stops, but her little booted foot taps impatiently until I draw alongside. "What's your name?" I ask.

She does an eye roll. "Is that all? It's Gabby."

I blink. "Gabby?"

"Yes. It's short for Gabriel, but my mom always says Gabby suits me better because I talk so much. What's your name?"

"Abby," I tell her.

She hoots with laughter. "That's funny! We rhyme. Is Abby short for something?"

"Yes," I say. "Abigail."

"Hey," she says, "that almost rhymes too! Well, are you coming? I want to brush Sugar and give him his apple. And I brought some sparkles to put in his mane. Don't you think he'll look beautiful with sparkles?"

She goes on, talking a mile a minute. It's hard to keep up with the river of chatter after being in Charlie's quiet presence. His presence. That reminds me of something I heard a lifetime ago. Mrs. Green, in group therapy, spoke about this as a quality we need.

I push the thought aside and try to keep pace with Gabby. But when I get to the alcove to watch her lesson, the thought comes back. Taylor has presence. There is no way anyone looks past Taylor. Charlie has it. Sugar. Even chatty Gabby, who can't be more than eight years old. She got it back. What is it that gives them this? They must feel right with themselves. I still don't feel right with myself. Why?

I've been asking myself this, straight out, ever since that first ride on Charlie. I think I'm being honest with myself, admitting I was an awful person. Isn't that important, honesty? That helped me figure out part of what I need. It's something very special and it's not legs. It's an obvious thing. It's what Sugar gave to Gabby, after she hit him. I've been afraid to ask for it. In case I don't get it.

Spiral

I look at Gabby trotting around on Sugar and think about how much courage it must have taken for her to come back. I needed courage too, to get on Charlie. I can do this.

I write a long-overdue letter to my parents. I tell them about riding Charlie, about the work, about Taylor's boyfriend. I tell them I'm getting stronger and that someday I hope to ride as well as Taylor. She is amazing to watch. It's as if she becomes one with the horse. She thinks I'll be better than her if I keep working hard.

I don't tell them about Gabby. But I do write: *I am so thankful you sent me to Spiral. I don't know how I can ever repay you, but I will. And I'm sorry for what I did. So sorry.*

I write a letter to Lily. I tell her many of the same things, but add this: *Thank you for standing by me, Lily.*

I wish I could have told you about the crap coke, and I'm sorry now that I didn't. I was a fool. And thanks for telling me the truth. I was such a baby about my injury. I don't know how you put up with me. Please say hi to Todd and everyone else for me.

I write one more, to Will. *Hey, Will. You were right, I was mean to you. Being a druggie freak made me even nastier than ever. I'm not mad at you for ratting on me. You did the right thing. Thanks, kiddo. Miss you.*

I sign all the letters: *Love, Abby.*

I give them to Dr. Scott for her to put in the mail. Then I go talk to Charlie. He listens, with both ears tilted my way. "I need their forgiveness, Charlie. That's a big part of it. If they can do that for me, I think maybe, someday, I can forgive myself."

Spiral

I never truly leave Spiral. The day does come when I go home to my family and start over with them. It isn't easy at first, but we manage. Their forgiveness is far bigger than the little I find for myself. Their trust? That takes longer. I go out with Lily. I return to school. I get another job, sorting books at the library.

The beast isn't entirely dead. But I keep it locked in a cage with bars built of the desire to live. To grow. To learn. It takes a long time before I learn how to feel right with myself. I never get there by aiming straight at it. I get there in a roundabout way.

The solution was all around me at Spiral. It was in the place and the people. Mostly, it was in the horses, the beings that form a circle around their young and keep them safe in the center. It takes many more weekends at Spiral to find what I seek. I muck out stalls. I keep riding. Taylor teaches me all she knows about the art of dressage, that fancy French word that simply means "training."

I soak it up, and one day Taylor says, "Abby, I can't teach you any more. From here on, it's just you and Charlie. You two go ahead and dance."

And we do. It's as if, with every stage of my learning, Charlie has been way ahead of me. But when we attempt an advanced pattern of movements, a "test" Taylor calls it, he becomes someone else. Charlie, the Master. He demands that I am on cue. He won't accept anything less. He wants an equal. I know that he'll do all I ask, but the question must be put properly.

The world narrows to this. I put my entire self into the test. And when I get the questions right, he gives me the answers I seek. He performs every difficult movement. His steps rise and float. His reach is longer. He is talented and awesome in his strength. He flaunts his presence with his neck arched proudly, his eyes alight.

When we're done, I've got it too. He drew it out of me.

It's about being in harmony. Mind, body, spirit all working as one. Yes, I am flawed, but that's the way it is. I don't need perfection. I just need to stay in the center.

Acknowledgments

As always, I am grateful to the members of my writing group, Shelley Hrdlitschka and Diane Tullson; they are the best of companions for this journey. I also wish to thank Hannah Denman for reading *Spiral* and providing insightful comment. And for all the horses I have been privileged to know, my gratitude for the wisdom and joy they've shared through simply *being* is beyond words.

K.L. Denman is the author of a number of novels from Orca, including *Mirror Image* and *The Shade*. She lives on British Columbia's Sunshine Coast.

orca soundings

For more information on all the books
in the Orca Soundings series, please visit
www.orcabook.com.